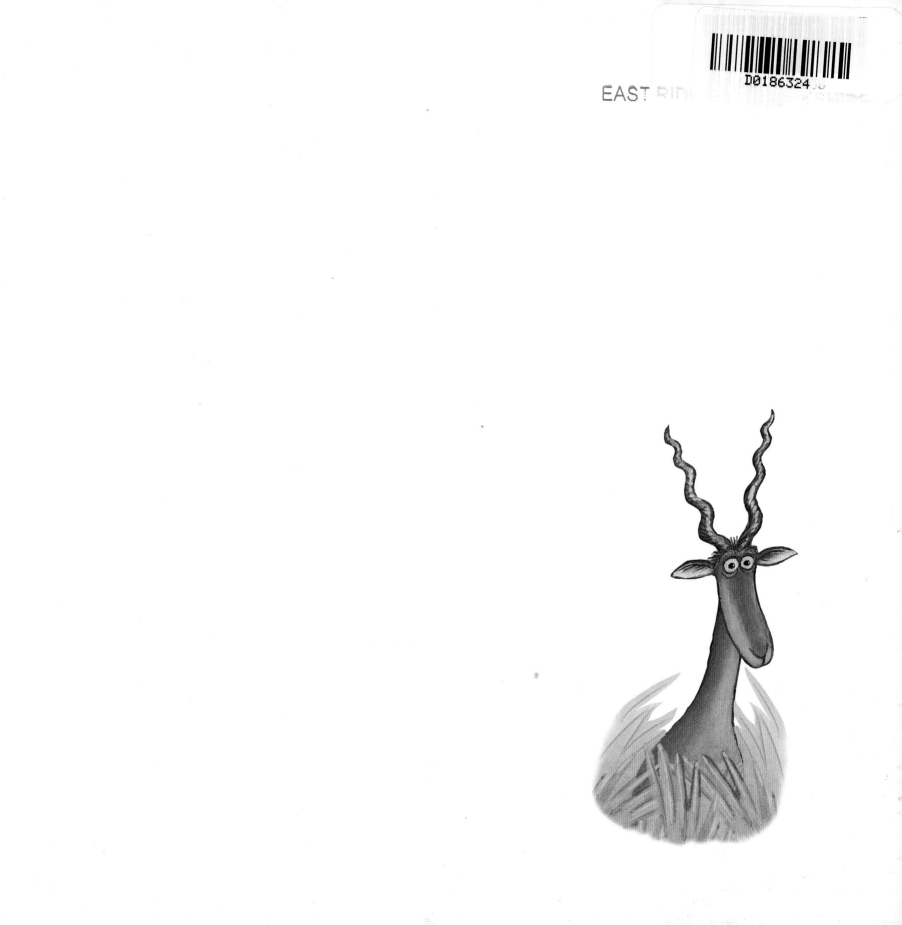

To my daughter Kysha — F.C.

To my son Jamie — M.T.

BLOOMSBURY CHILDREN'S BOOKS
Bloomsbury Publishing Plc
50 Bedford Square, London, WC1B 3DP, UK

BLOOMSBURY, BLOOMSBURY CHILDREN'S BOOKS and the Diana logo are trademarks of Bloomsbury Publishing Plc

First published in Great Britain 1998 by Bloomsbury Publishing Plc
This edition published in 2018 by Bloomsbury publishing Plc

A catalogue record for this book is available from the British Library

ISBN: PB: 978-1-4088-8525-3; PB and CD: 978-1-4088-9761-4

2 4 6 8 10 9 7 5 3 1 (paperback)
2 4 6 8 10 9 7 5 3 1 (paperback and CD)

Designed by Dawn Apperley

Printed and bound in China by RR Donnelley Asia Printing Solutions Limited

All papers used by Bloomsbury Publishing Plc are natural, recyclable products from wood grown in well managed forests. The manufacturing processes conform to the environmental regulations of the country of origin

To find out more about our authors and books visit www.bloomsbury.com and sign up for our newsletters

THE
SELFISH CROCODILE

Faustin Charles and Michael Terry

BLOOMSBURY
CHILDREN'S BOOKS
LONDON OXFORD NEW YORK NEW DELHI SYDNEY

Deep in the forest, in the river, lived a large crocodile. He was a very selfish crocodile. He didn't want any other creature to drink or bathe in the river. He thought it was HIS river.

Every day, he shouted to the creatures of the forest, 'Stay away from my river! It's MY river! If you come in my river, I'll eat you all!'

So there were no fish, no tadpoles, no frogs, no crabs, no crayfish in the river. All were afraid of the selfish crocodile.

The forest creatures kept away from the river as well. Whenever they were thirsty, they went for miles to drink in other rivers and streams.

Every day the crocodile lay on his great big back in the sun, picking his big, sharp teeth with a stick.

But early one morning, the forest was awakened by a loud groaning sound. Something was in terrible pain.

The creatures thought that it was an animal caught by the crocodile.

GROAN

But as the sun came out brightly, they saw that it was the crocodile who was in pain. He was lying on his big back, holding his swollen jaw, and he was crying real tears.

GROAN

The creatures drew closer – but not too close. Some of the creatures felt sorry for the crocodile.

'What's the matter with him?' asked a deer.

'I don't know,' said a squirrel.

'Maybe he's going to die,' chirped a bird.

'If that happens it'll be safe to go in the river!' grunted a wild pig.

The animals thought about this. They hung from branches, they hung from vines; they buzzed in the air, and they shook their heads as they watched the great big crocodile in pain. No animal tried to help.

Suddenly a little mouse appeared, sniffing the air.
He ran along the crocodile's tail, then on to his tummy.
The other creatures stared.

'Look at that mouse!' chattered a monkey.

'He's either very brave or mad!'

'He's going to be eaten for sure!' said an iguana.

The mouse crept along the crocodile's big neck, and into his open mouth.

There was a hush in the forest.

The mouse got hold of something, and pulled and pulled and pulled. Then he put it on his shoulder and walked out of the crocodile's mouth.

There was a loud cheer from the astonished creatures.

He told them that he was worried in case he got lost…

or started to cry.

He told the birds that his mum had bought him new shoes with difficult laces.

"I wish I was a bird," said Billy. "Then I wouldn't have to worry about school at all. Or shoelaces."

Suddenly the birds started making a terrible noise.
Billy saw a new bird sitting on the ground. It was a tiny
sparrow. All the other birds were picking on it and
trying to chase it away.

But the little sparrow couldn't fly properly. It wasn't
really ready to look after itself.

It was the smallest, grubbiest, weediest, most dusty bird
Billy had ever seen. Billy called his mum.
    Billy's mum ran out and chased the other birds away.
Then they carried the little sparrow inside.

The kitchen was warm, but
the sparrow was shivering.
Billy found the box from his
new shoes.

He made a bed of cotton wool
and put the bird gently inside.
He could feel its little heart
beating.

Then Billy gave the bird a bowl
of water and a tiny piece of
bread, but it wasn't hungry.

So Billy sat and talked gently
to the sparrow.

All that Sunday the sparrow lay in the box and watched Billy with a big round eye.

And all that same Sunday Billy's mum got things ready
for the next day at the new school.

She wrote his name *Billy* on his clothes…   his bag…

his pencil case…   and the new shoes with the difficult laces.

That night, Billy had a scary dream. He dreamt that
he was a little bird who couldn't fly and the other birds
were picking on him.

Then his mum came in to the bedroom and gave
him a big hug. And Billy felt better.

In the morning, Billy woke up so early for school that it was still dark.

He had forgotten all about the little sparrow, until he walked into the kitchen and saw it sitting in the middle of the floor. It had hopped out of the shoe box all by itself.

"It must be feeling better," said Billy's mum. "I think it's time to let it go."

The bird had to go into the big world – just like Billy.

So Billy gently picked up the little bird and opened the window.

"You have to fly away," he whispered. "You have to learn to look after yourself like me."

The little bird looked up at Billy. It seemed to understand. Suddenly it hopped onto the windowsill and flew away into the sky.

After breakfast Billy took his new bag
and his mum helped him with his shoelaces.

Then it was time for school.

Billy's teacher was called Mrs Berry.
She was very nice.

She showed Billy where
to hang his coat…

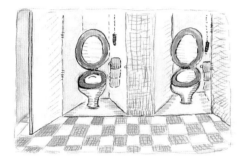

and where the
toilets were…

and the sink to
wash his hands…

and the paints…

and the computer…

and the playhouse…

and the reading corner.
Billy even found a big
book all about birds.

Some other children were new as well.

After a while, another boy came and looked at Billy's book too. Then Billy had a friend.

After lunch Mrs Berry talked to the class about animals. She asked if anyone had a pet.

Daisy had a dog.

Callum had a cat.

Jeremy had a gerbil.

Wendy had a worm.

Tom and Maddy, the twins, had a tortoise.
Billy was very interested.

"What about you, Billy?" asked Mrs Berry.

Billy thought for a moment. Then slowly he stood up.

In a tiny voice he began to tell everyone all about his bird table. Then he told them about the poor little sparrow. And about how he had put it in a shoe box until it was ready to fly...

When he had finished the story Mrs Berry began to clap.
And so did all the big children in Billy's class. Then Billy sat down.
His face was bright red. But his smile was the biggest in the school.

That night, Billy had another dream. But this one wasn't scary at all. He dreamt he could fly over the house, over the garden, over the town, and way over the big school, just like a bird. Billy and the birds flew high above the world and turned somersaults over the moon.

A few days later, Billy brought his new friend home from school.

They rolled about in the garden and got all dirty.
But Billy's mum didn't mind.

Billy and his friend had a picnic. They were very hungry.
All the birds came looking for crumbs.

Suddenly Billy saw one bird that looked almost exactly like the
sparrow from the shoe box. But he couldn't be quite sure because
this sparrow was bigger, and this sparrow was braver, and this sparrow
was happier, and this sparrow had lots of friends.

JUST LIKE BILLY.